Hazel's Great Adventure

....

Hazel's Great Adventure

by a Dog Called Hazel

translated by

James R. Olsen

Breaking Wave Publishing

Breaking Wave Publishing
Hamilton, Montana
www.BreakingWavePublishing.com

www.JamesROlsen.com

Library of Congress Control Number: 2024923174.
Olsen, James R.
Hazel's Great Adventure

ISBN: 978-1-7342332-4-7

Printed in the United States of America
3 4 5 6 7 8 9 10

Cover by James R. Olsen

Dedicated to
Tom and Sue Cratty

Can dogs love? Can dogs have a broken heart? My answer is yes. How do we know? I respond with the question: How do we know people love? We feel it. We describe it, tell stories about it, and tell people when we feel it. Even so, when there are no words, we see two people and say, "They love each other." This is what I attempt in this book, to take a particular dog's actions and expressions and give words to them as best I can. The events are true, the dog called Hazel's words are my guess.

Even though Hazel doesn't know place names, I use them to orient the readers; she does know if she has been there before and in what context. The same goes for cars. Hazel does know what action her tribe desires of her for certain words and gestures. She is very attentive to patterns, gestures, and sounds. Her world is full of smells, with all of their nuances and differentiation. She can tell the difference between a lizard and a squirrel; can identify each individual person and dog. She differentiates the smell of different animals, so I name them for the reader. I use the nouns and pronouns familiar to the reader.

I interpret Hazel's emotions from how she behaves, how attentive or listless, rambunctious or cautious as I watch her or, on occasion, view cabin footage from the Tesla. There is a lot of guesswork. I watch her move, walk, trot, pace, canter, gallop, and what I call the squirrel sprint — a blur of white and brown fur — I wouldn't want to be that squirrel.

How would Hazel tell us a story? When I contemplated this, her words often came forth from the keyboard in poetic prose. Maybe call it dog verse.

My wife, Mary, and I care for Hazel. Hazel is eight, a Jack Russell Terrier, raised with a non-sibling male Jack Russel. We took her into our care this year and went on a road trip with Hazel in a Blue Tesla. A Tesla has Dog Mode — if we need to leave Hazel alone, we thought it best to use the car instead of some strange hotel room.

Hazel lost all three of the people who cared for her last year, two passed away, and one had to move away. Of course, for Hazel, there was no closure. If someone said to Hazel that they would never come back, it was beyond Hazel's English vocabulary to understand it. She could only wait.

She was taken to a different house. The two dogs in their new home didn't get along that well. We were asked to take care of Hazel for a week, with the suggestion we could keep her — we didn't think so.

After a few days, Hazel weighed on my mind. I consulted the I Ching. After some contemplation, it suggested we "Care for the animal with the tears." I looked at her face — it was obvious — the brown tear-stained fur under her eyes laying over a white fur looked like tears. It was settled.

After settling into our routine for a month, Hazel notices us loading up the car. And so begins Hazel's Big Adventure.

A Dog Called Hazel tells her story.

Murray Hotel, Livingston, Montana, May 8, 2024

1. A New Home

They call me Hazel.

I am alone with new people. Is this my new home? Is this house and yard my new home? Are The Woman Who Feeds Me and the Man With Whom I Hunt my new family?

I grew up with The Man Who Trained Me, The Woman Who Fed Me, and the Woman Who Held Me On Her Lap — with them and a Dog Called Ozzy. The Dog Called Ozzy and I jump, run, jump when we meet. But I have to hurry to eat my food because the Dog Called Ozzy will rush over and eat it before I do.

We lived with Them, The Man Who Trained Me, The Woman Who Fed Me, and the Woman Who Held Me On Her Lap.

They left. I don't know why. I waited. I waited. I wait. They have not come back to me, The Man Who Trained

Me, The Woman Who Fed Me, The Woman Who Held Me On Her Lap.

Hamilton, Montana

The Man Who Builds Thing took Ozzy and me to a new house. I met new people. The Dog Called Ozzy and The Man Who Builds Things left.

Now I am alone with new people. Is this my new home? Is this house and yard my new home? Are The Woman Who Feeds Me and the Man With Whom I Hunt my new family? Now, when I rush to eat, the Dog Called Ozzy does not come to my bowl.

I lie here waiting. I wait. I wait. I think of them who have not came back, The Man Who Trained Me, The Woman Who Fed Me, The Woman Who Held Me On Her Lap. Tears in my heart.

I look out the window. Squirrels in the yard. Squirrels! I stand alert. I watch. Squirrels! I stand alert. I watch. The squirrels run behind bushes. Squirrels disappear up trees.

Is this my new home?

The Woman Who Feeds Me now Takes Me for Long Walks, the leash keeping me at her pace. There is comfort in that.

Now, The Man With Whom I Hunt points the way. We hunt, like with the Man Who Trained Me. But The Man With Whom I Now Hunt is different, different words, "This way," "Heel, Heel, Heel." New gestures, an arm raised, finger pointing.

I am cantering in the tall grass. I am trying to learn. I smell dogs who were here. I smell geese who were here. I smell deer who were here. I smell a raccoon who was here. I smell bugs in the grass. I stop. I smell. I trot. I canter. The grass brushes my fur, a soft stroke sweeping across my skin. We hunt, The Man With Whom I Hunt and me.

"Come," "Come," I trot to the Man. l am learning. I am learning the ways of the new family.

I lie here. I wait. I lie here in my new home. I have smelled it. I smell The Woman Who Feeds Me and The Man With Whom I Hunt in this home, everywhere in this home. I smell my own scent in this home. A Familiar Home. I eat. I drink. I smell my new home.

I look out the window. I see birds flying, walking, pecking in the grass. I lie here. I wait. I lie here in my new home. I sleep. I dream of the old hunts. I dream of those who have not come back, The Man Who Trained Me, The Woman Who Fed Me, The Woman Who Held Me On Her Lap. Tears in my heart.

2. THE BLUE CAR

Something is changing. The Woman and Man are putting stuff in the Blue Car. I have been in cars. They travel. They carry us in them. They are putting stuff in the Blue Car. They are going away in the car.

Take me with you. Take me with you. My place is with you. I jump in the Blue Car. Take me with you.

My heart beats fast. I jump to be with The Man With Whom I Hunt. I jump to be with The Woman Who Feeds Me, The

Woman Who Takes Me for Long Walks. I need to be with you. Take me with you. Where do I sit? I am going with you. Going with you. Going with you.

They dog-handled me to the back seat. I am with you. I am with you. I jump to be with the Woman, I jump to be with the Man. They put me on the console between them. They pet me. "Stay." Pet me. "Stay." "Stay."

I sit. I look around. I sit. I lie here.

The car moves. Buildings, trees, cars fly by the window. I lie on the console with them. I wait. I wait. The next thing will come — I don't need to know when. I'm with them. I wait. The car rocks and rumbles and rocks. I wait. I wait. I sleep.

Up Chief Joseph Pass, through the Big Hole, Montana

3. THE PARKING LOT

Rocker, Montana, White and Red Tesla Charging Stations

It is a strange sight. The Man With Whom I Hunt inserts a tail into the Blue Car.

The Woman Who Takes Me for Long Walks walks away. I watch where she goes. She disappears through a door. I watch. I watch. I watch.

The Man With Whom I Hunt motions. "Out." I jump down.

Around the White and Red Pillars I trot. The Blue Car rattles and hums. I pace around White and Red Pillars. The Blue Car purrs. I circle around The White and Red Pillars. The Pillars hum. The Blue Car hums. I trot around the car.

Then I remember. I look at where she went. She is not here. I worry.

"This way." I trot to the grass and bushes. I smell, I scout, I watch, I scout, I smell. They have been here, a dog, a bug, a dog, a cat, bugs, bugs. I trot. My knee in my back leg slips. I lift it in a skip. It's fixed. I trot. A mouse, I follow the trail, nose to the ground, I smell. I hunt.

I look at where she went.

She is walking back. Here she comes. To me. Here she comes. To me. I jump for joy. I jump. I jump. I jump. I lick.

"Up," says the man. In the car I go. The car moves. Buildings, trees, cars, fly by the window. I lie on the console with them. I wait. I wait. The next thing will come — I don't need to know when. I'm with them. I wait. The car rocks and rumbles and rock. I wait. I wait. I sleep. I remember, The Man Who Trained Me, The Woman Who Fed Me, The Woman Who Held Me On Her Lap. Tears in my heart.

Through Butte, Bozeman, Montana

4. THE ELEVATOR

Livingston, Montana, Murray Hotel

The Blue Car stops. We are still. I look out the windows. Cars going by on one side. People on the sidewalk saunter by. The wind blows; the train cars clatter. The Man and Woman get stuff out of the car. Are we staying here? Are we staying here?

"Out." I am on the leash. I see people. I see cars.

A door with a glass pane. I smell the scents coming under the door. I put my front paws on the window. I look through. I like this window. I like this window in the door.

The door opens, we go through. I am on the leash. The people are pulling stuff. A tile floor and more people. I meet another dog. We sniff each other.

I sit next to the stuff. I look around. I wait.

The Woman With Keys walks from behind the counter. The Man With Whom I Hunt and The Woman Who Takes Me for Long Walks pull the stuff. I am on the leash but am not sure where to go. I am tugged this way.

A few steps to another door, a metal door. The Woman With Keys opens the metal door. A little room. The Woman and the Man put the stuff in the room. The Man With Whom I Hunt motions. I go in the little room.

Legs all around me. I look up. The room moves! The room goes up. Up, rattle, up. I am nervous — a moving room. I brace myself. Up, rattle, up. Rattle. The room stops.

The door opens. "Out." We walk, the Man With Whom I Hunt and The Woman Who Feeds Me pull stuff.

We are in a big room with a bed, couch, and furniture. I smell, I smell, I inspect. Is this our new home? I jump on the couch. I lie down. I watch. I wait. I'm with them in a new den. Our new den. I wait. I wait. The next thing will come — I don't need to know when. I'm with them. I wait.

5. WINDOW SHOPPING

Livingston, Montana

I am on the leash. I trot around town. The wind blows across my fur, a soft stroke rippling across my skin. I see, I hear, I smell people, cars, doors with windows. New smells, new sights. The Man With Whom I Hunt walks, I trot, along the sidewalk. The sidewalk is wet with rain.

I stop at a door. I smell the scents coming under the door. I like to look in the windows in doors. I see stuff inside. We walk. I stop at each door. I smell. I look.

I stop and look at something on the sidewalk. It looks like a little donkey. Its head is bobbing up and down. I don't get too close. I sniff. It doesn't smell like an animal. That makes me cautious.

A street with lots of cars. "Heel." Heel." "Heel." We cross the street. I am off the leash. I am in the grass. I smell. I smell dogs that were once here. I smell bugs. I look up. I see big metal cars hooked together. They rattle, clatter. The big metal cars whistle loudly.

6. THE PARK

Livingston, Montana, Sacajawea Park

There are interesting birds, ducks, geese. I am on the leash. The Woman Who Takes Me For Long Walks is walking. I trot. The cold wind blows across my fur. I see, I hear, I hear the water running in the river.

A car stops. A dog looks out the window, a dog like me. The Woman Who Takes Me for Long Walks greets the people in the car. The car travels on. She walks, I trot.

It's raining. I'm wet. I'm cold. I shiver. I trot. I trot through the wet grass. I shiver. We turn around.

We walk to the Blue Car. The Man With Whom I Hunt opens the door. "Up." I jump up in the Blue Car. It is warm.

Livingston, Montana, Murray Hotel

We are at door with the window I like. We walk past the door to The Little Room That Goes Up. I see stairs.

The Man With Whom I Hunt says, "Up." Up the stairs I go. I canter. Up the stairs, I canter. I canter up. I canter up. I get to a flat spot. "Up." Up the stairs I go. I get to the top.

"This way." Down a hall, to a door. The man opens the door We are in the big room. It is warm. It has nice couches and chairs. The man and woman gets me water and food. I eat.

The Woman Who Feeds Me and The Man With Whom I Hunt sleep in the bed. I sleep with them. I curl up in a dog ball. I sleep. I sleep.

I dream. I remember. I remember, The Man Who Trained Me, The Woman Who Fed Me, The Woman Who Held Me On Her Lap. Tears in my heart.

7. THE STORM

The Woman and Man wake up. They are putting stuff in the Blue Car. The wind is blowing. The rain hits my fur. I am on the sidewalk, watching.

They are going away in the car — take me with you. Take me with you. My place is with you. "Up." I jump in the car. I am in the seat. The Woman Who Takes Me for Long

Walks opens the door. "Get in your go place." "Your go place." Hands put me on the console.

Billings, Montana

The car travels and travels. I see snow blowing by the windows. I see snow on the ground. I hear the wind hitting the car. I feel the Blue Car shaking. I see snow, car shapes and tree shadows.

A Parking Lot

"Out." Snow falls on me. I trot through the cold mush. I don't like to get my paws wet. The air is cold. The slush is cold. The air is cold. I can't smell much. I am cold. I am wet. I shiver.

The car door opens. "Up." The man rubs me with a towel. I shiver. The Blue Car blows warm air on me. I shiver. Warm air. I stop shivering.

The Blue Car travels. The gentle rocking is soothing. I lay on the console. The vibration on my belly. The Blue Car travels. I remember those who never came back. I sleep. The car rocks. I sleep.

I dream of those who never came back, The Man Who Trained Me, The Woman Who Fed Me, The Woman Who Held Me On Her Lap. Tears in my heart.

I wake up. I look out the window. I see fields covered with snow. Brown grass blades stick up through the snow. There are mountains, gray rocks and white snow.

It is cold and gray. I wait. They never came back. I wait. Will the Woman Who Feeds Me and The Man With Whom I Hunt leave me? I fear. Will they leave me forever? I wait.

8. Alice's Restaurant

Big Horn, Wyoming, Mary's Sister Alice's House

We stop. "Out." They get stuff out of the Blue Car. A door to a new home. A Woman greets me. I am in a warm home. There is a Dog Called Peppy, my size dog. The Woman gives me a treat. I am welcome. I and the Dog Called Peppy run around in the yard. Joy. We eat at our bowls.

I stand on the back of a chair and look out the big picture window. I see trees. I see birds. I look for squirrels.

The Woman gives treats. She gives the Dog Called Peppy treats. A good place this.

It is her place on the couch, The Woman Who Gives Treats. The Dog Called Peppy often sits beside her. But The Dog Called Peppy is not here. I hop up. A treat. Is this my treat place?

The Dog Called Peppy approaches. My treat place. My treat place. I growl a little. My treat place. The Woman Who Gives Treats gives us both a treat.

The Woman Who Feeds Me and The Man With Whom I Hunt sleep in the bed. I sleep with them, curled up in a dog ball. I sleep. I sleep. I dream. I remember. I remember those who never came back, The Man Who Trained Me, The Woman Who Fed Me, The Woman Who Held Me On Her Lap. Tears in my heart.

Another day. We eat, me and the Dog Called Peppy. We run through the house. We go out in the yard. I smell deer. The deer smell is strong, they visit often.

More treats. Another night. This is a good place. I sleep. I curl up in a dog ball.

9. FROM THE MOUNTAINS TO THE PLAINS

The woman and man put stuff in the Blue Car. Are we leaving? Are we leaving? I lick. "Up." We are traveling.

We travel. We stop. I eat, I poop, I hunt. We stop.

Cheyenne, Wyoming

I smell. I inspect a new parking lot. I inspect a big boot. I eat, I poop, I hunt. I lie in a new bed.

I dream of the joy of hunt with The Man Who Trained Me, the kindness of The Woman Who Fed Me and The Woman Who Held Me On Her Lap. Tears in my heart.

Russell, Kansas

The Blue Car travels across the plains. I look out the windows.

When we stop, sometimes The Woman Who Takes Me for Long Walks leaves. I watch. I watch. I watch. I see her come back to the Blue Car. I jump for joy, I jump. I lick. Sometimes,

The Man With Whom I Hunt leaves. I watch. I watch. I watch. I see him come back to the Blue Car. I jump for joy. I jump. I lick.

The Blue Car stops. White and Red Pillars. They both leave me, The Woman Who Takes Me for Long Walks and the Man With Whom I Hunt walk away.

I am in the car alone. I am in the car alone. Will they come back? Will they come back? I look out the window. I look. I look. I look. My heart is beating fast. My heart beating fast. I am panting.

I see them. Walking toward me. I jump. I bark. I jump. I bark. The door of the Blue Car opens. My heart is beating fast. I pant. The Woman Who Takes Me for Long Walks pets me. My heart beats fast. They left me. They left me. They left me. My heart beats fast. My heart beats fast.

The Man With Whom I Hunt says, "Out." I am in the grass. I am in the bushes. The bushes rub against my sides. "This way." I hunt. I smell. I hunt. They have been here, dogs, mice, birds. My heart slows.

I hunt. I smell. A squirrel scent. I trot. I am on the scent. I pace. I am on the scent. I stop. The squirrel scent. I trot. I am on the scent. I stop. I turn. The squirrel scent is this way. I walk, nose to the grounds. I smell.

"Come." I smell. I walk. "Come." I am on the squirrel scent. "Come." "Come." I stop. I look up. I must go. I trot to The Man With Whom I Hunt.

10. GOPHERS

Wichita, Kansas

"Out." I am it a field of short grass with holes dug in them. I smell. I smell. I smell gophers under the ground. I go from hole to hold and smell. I can't see them, but I smell them. I trot away.

11. THE BIG, BIG DOG

Stillwater, Oklahoma

A new house. I meet The Woman Who Cooks. I meet the Dog Called Pete. The Dog Called Pete is a big, big dog.

I lay on the couch. The Dog Called Pete rests his chin on the couch. I am nervous. The Dog Called Pete moves slowly. That is good.

I sit on the lap of The Woman Who Feeds Me. The Dog Called Pete comes toward me, toward The Woman Who Feeds Me, his head looking down at me. I growl softly. The Dog Called Pete moves away.

"Walk." We go for a walk. The Man With Whom I Hunt guides the way. "This way Hazel." When we cross the street, "Heel… heel…" I know I'm supposed to stay close, the left, but not sure exactly where. "Heel." I am trying to learn.

Grass and bushes, I smell. I hunt. I hunt. I hunt. This is who I am. This is who I am. This is who I am. A smell, a squirrel smell, I stop. I smell, I track. I track. I track. I stop. The people are far away.

"Come." The squirrel The squirrel smell. I don't want to leave the squirrel smell. "Come, Come, Come." I leave the hunt, nose to the ground. I walk slowly. "Come. Come."

I see The Man With Whom I Hunt, I gallop. With every muscle I gallop. A joy. A joy, I am with them. I am with them.

We sleep. The sun shines through the window. I wake up. I eat. I am on the leash. The Woman Who Takes Me for Long Walks, The Man With Whom I Hunt, The Woman Who Cooks, and The Dog Called Pete walk on the street.

We walk on the sidewalks. Another woman waves. We Stop. Two Dogs. I am off the leash in an new back yard. There is a pond.

The Two Dogs jump in the water. The Dog Called Pete jumps in the water. I don't want to jump in the water. I smell. I smell. I hunt in the bushes. I don't want to jump in the water with the big dogs.

The Woman Who Cooks cooks. People eat. The Dog Called Pete eats. I eat.

They put stuff in the Blue Car. We travel. We stop. I eat, I poop, I hunt. We stop. I eat, I poop, I hunt, I lie in a new bed. Sometimes the Woman or Man leaves. I watch. I watch. When The Woman Who Takes Me for Long Walks comes back to the Blue Car, I jump for joy. When The Man With Whom I Hunt comes back to the Blue Car, I jump for joy.

Round Rock, Texas

I lie in a new bed. I dream of the hunt with The Man Who Trained Me, the kindness of The Woman Who Fed Me and The Woman Who Held Me On Her Lap. Tears in my heart. They never came back.

12. THE LONG GOODBYE

Shadows are getting long. "Up." I jump into the Blue Car. We travel.

Lake Travis, Texas, Oasis Restaurant Parking Lot

The Blue Car stops. Cars, cars, cars everywhere. The Woman Who Takes Me for Long Walks and The Man With Whom I Hunt walk away. I am in the Blue Car alone. I look out the window. I look. I look. Other people around me. I am here. I am here. I am here. I bark. I bark. I bark. The other people do not come to me.

I wait. I wait. I wait. How soon will they come back? I am alone in the Blue Car, cars all around me. I wait.

It gets dark. I bark. I bark. I bark. Come get me. Come get me. Come get me. I press against the window. I press against the window. I jump. I look. I jump. I look. I jump. I look. I am alone. No one comes.

I try to calm down. I lie here. I wait. I wait. I wait. I am alone. How soon will they come back?

I can't wait. I can't wait. I can't wait. I look. I jump. I look. I jump. I look. I am alone. No one comes. I am alone. In the Blue Car. Is the Blue Car my new home? But I am alone. I am alone. I am alone. I jump. I look. I bark. I jump. I look. I pant. I jump. I look. I bark. I am alone. Come to me, The Woman Who Feeds Me and the Man With Whom I Hunt. Come get me. Come get me.

I try to calm down. I lie here. I wait. I wait. I wait. I am alone. Will they come back? It's too long. It's too long.
Come to me, The Woman Who Feeds Me, The Man With Whom I Hunt, The Man Who Trained Me, The Woman

Who Fed Me, The Woman Who Held Me On Her Lap. They are gone. They are gone. They are gone.

I am alone. My heart beats fast. My heart beats faster. My heart beats faster. I look. I jump. I call them. I bark. I bark. I bark. I am alone. Oh, oh, bursting tears in my heart. They are not coming back. They are not coming back.

In the Blue Car. I cannot get out. I cannot look for them. Will I be alone forever? My heart beats faster. My heart beats faster. My heart beats faster. They are gone, The Woman Who Feeds Me, the Man With Whom I Hunt, The Man Who Trained Me, The Woman Who Fed Me, The Woman Who Held Me On Her Lap. My heart is pounding, pounding, pounding. Unbearable fear in my heart.

I lie down. I wait. I try to lie down. I try to wait. I can't wait. I look. I jump. I look. I jump. I look. I am alone. They are not coming back. They are not coming back, The Woman Who Feeds Me, The Man With Whom I Hunt, The Man Who Trained Me, The Woman Who Fed Me, The Woman Who Held Me On Her Lap. My heart is pounding, pounding, pounding. Unbearable tears in my heart.

I see a man. It is The Man With Whom I Hunt! I jump. I bark. I jump. I bark. I jump. I bark. I am here. I am here. I am here. I am here. The Man With Whom I Hunt opens the door. I jump. I jump for joy. I jump. I lick. I jump. I lick. He holds me. He holds me. My heart is pounding, pounding, pounding. He holds me. He pets me. My heart is pounding,

pounding, pounding. I can't calm down. I pant. I can't calm down. I pant. I can't calm down. I pant.

He carries me to the grass. He puts me down.

"This way." The grass edge of the parking lot. "This way." I trot. I hunt. I hunt. This is who I am. This is who I am. This is who I am. I hunt in the bushes. I smell the mice who were once here. I hunt. I hunt. My heart slows. This is who I am. This is who I am. This is who I am.

I hunt. I hunt. I hunt with The Man With Whom I Hunt. This is who I am. This is who I am. This is who I am.

The Woman Who Feeds Me, The Man With Whom I Hunt came back. They are with me, The Woman Who Feeds Me, The Man With Whom I Hunt.

I hunt in the night. This is who I am. This is who I am. This is who I am. My hunting heart is bright, hunting in the night. My hunting heart is bright.

"Up." Their smell is always here, in the Blue Car.

13. LIZARDS

Victoria, Texas, Tesla Charging Station

The Blue Car is where I am with them, The Woman Who Takes Me for Long Walks, The Man With Whom I Hunt. Is the Blue Car my new home?

We stop. The Blue Car. "Out." I hunt. I smell. I smell something new. I stick my nose in the bushes. My whiskers feel a rock. I turn my head.

I see the flash of a lizard. I smell the lizard. It scuttles. I rustle the bushes. I stick my nose in the bushes. I hunt. It scuttles. I jump. I miss. This is who I am. This is who I am. This is who I am. Lizards scuttle. I jump. Scuttle. I stick my nose in the bushes. Scuttle. Too fast for me — this time.

14. A Beach Cabin on the Sand

Port Aransas, Texas, Air bnb Cabins

We stop. "Out." I am on the sand. I see a blue porch. I see cabins. I see people. I smell. I smell The Woman Who Has a Dog, The Man Who Smells Like The Texas Hills, The Woman Who Smiles Brightly, The Man With Music, The Woman Who Takes Me for Long Walks, The Man With

Whom I Hunt. They pet me. They welcome me. I inspect my new home.

I run around in the yard. I feel the gentle touch of warm breeze. I smell the sand. I smell the creatures of the sand, a bug, a mouse, a bug, a lizard, a cat, a bug, a dog. I eat. I drink. I smell the critters in the sand. "Come." "Come." "Come." I trot to the cabin.

They pet me, The Woman Who Has a Dog, The Man Who Smells Like The Texas Hills, The Woman Who Smiles Brightly, The Man With Music In His Soul.

15. Wood, Sand, and Thorns

North Padre Island, Packery Channel Oak Motte Sanctuary, Audubon Outdoor Club of Corpus Christi.

"Out." It is hot. The cars have stopped. The people walk up a wooden path. The Woman Who Takes Me for Long Walks picks me up and carries me along a wooden path and puts me down.

I am standing on wood, trees all around me. The air is still, damp, and hot. I go down three stairs into the sand, grass, and bushes. I smell birds. I smell the tracks of lizards. I watch for thorns as I walk the sandy path.

16. LIZARDS IN THE SIGN

We are back at the Blue Car. "Up." I jump in the car. "In your go place." I lie on the console. The Blue Car travels in road, over bridges, to a parking lot. "Out."

Corpus Christi, Texas, Hans and Pat Suter Wildlife Refuge

I am on the leash. I smell. I smell lizards. A lizard rushes up the back of a tall sign.

The lizards are up in the sign. I jump. I bark. Lizards. I jump. The lizards stay hidden in the sign. I jump. I jump high and hit my nose on the sign. The lizards escape —this time.

We walk along a wooden path, over grass, mud, and water. People hold things up to their eyes. I meet a dog.

I see birds in the bushes. I see birds standing in the mud. I see birds standing in the water. I see birds floating on the water. I see birds flying in the air.

The smell of the mud and the rotting grass. I smell creatures who live in shells and detect the scents of the of birds I see.

A wind blows back my fur.

17. REMEMBER (WALKING IN THE SAND)

Port Aransas, Texas, the beach

I am in the sand. My paws are sandy. The wind is blowing. My fur is ruffling. I smell the salt air. Smells, winds, waves. It is new. I remember my puppy days, the excitement when it was all new, The Man Who Trained Me, The Woman Who Fed Me, and the Woman Who Held Me On Her Lap.

The waves are coming. The waves are coming. The Woman Who Has a Dog runs from the waves. I run with her.

The Man With Whom I Hunt is in the water. "Come." I stay on the beach. "Come." I don't want to get in the water. I like the beach. I don't want be in the water. I don't want be in over my head and have to swim in the waves.

The Man With Whom I Hunt comes out of the water. He pours fresh water in my portable water bowl. I am thirsty. I drink.

I smell. I smell. I smell the sand crabs under the sand. I smell the birds running in front of the waves like me. I smell the spray of the water waves. I smell fish in the sea. The wind is ruffling through my fur. I am walking in the sand.

18. STRANGE BEASTS OF THE SEA

Port Aransas, Texas, Roberts Point Park and Ship Channel

"Out." The Blue Car. I am in a parking lot, on the grass. I smell dogs. I smell birds. I smell old mouse tracks. I smell grass. I smell bugs. I smell salt in the air. I hunt. I hunt. This is who I am. This is who I am. This is who I am. I smell fish. I see boats.

I see a big, big ship. I see dolphins, strange beasts of the sea. I cannot smell them, so I hunt in the grass. I hunt.

19. THE WAVES

Port Aransas, Texas, the beach

"Out." The Blue Car. I'm in the sand. I see the waves. It is hot. I pant. I pant. The Man With Whom I Hunt motions for me to walk in the waves. The waves make my nervous. I hesitate. I stop. I don't want to go in the waves.

The Man With Whom I Hunt picks me up and carries me into the waves. I trust him. He puts me down. I stand in the waves. The water rushes over my back. The waves wash over me. I am in the water. The waves wash over me.

The Man With Whom I Hunt puts me back on the sand. I am cooler now. I shake. I shake. I shake.

The wind is blowing. The waves washing up the beach. I trot. I pace. I gallop in the wind. Joy. I gallop in the wind to The Man With Whom I Hunt. He jumps. I sprint away.

I turn. I gallop in the wind. Joy. I gallop in the wind to The Man With Whom I Hunt.

The days and nights go by. I go for walks. I go to the beach. I eat. I walk around in the sand. The Woman Who Takes Me for Long Walks and The Man With Whom I Hunt sleep in the bed. I sleep with them, curled up in a dog ball. I sleep. I sleep. I dream. I remember.

I remember, The Man Who Trained Me, The Woman Who Fed Me, The Woman Who Held Me On Her Lap. Tears in my heart.

20. Nuts

The man and woman put stuff in the Blue Car. "Up." I jump in the car. "In your go place. In your go place." I sit on the console, and the Blue Car goes. I lie here.

Lulu, Texas, roadside stand, pecans

We stop. The Blue Car. "Stay." The Woman Who Takes Me for Long Walks, The Man With Whom I Hunt go through a door. I watch, I wait. I wait. My heart starts to beat fast. I watch.

They come out of the door. They come to me. "Out." Joyous greeting. I jump. I lick. "This way." The smells have changed, the critters of the trees, bushes, and grass.

In a parking lot, I hunt. I smell dogs that were here. In the alley I hunt. I smell mice, squirrels, cats, raccoons there were here. Along wall of the building. I hunt. This is who I am. This is who I am. This is who I am.

"Up." In the car I go. In my go place. The car travels. I lie on the console. I remember the beach, the wind, the sand, the waves and the sea creatures that I could smell but could not see.

21. A Place Where People Come and Go

Austin Airport

We stop at a busy street. Cars, people, stuff everywhere. I smell a woman I know, The Woman Who I Remember, the woman who visited the The Man Who Trained Me, The

Woman Who Fed Me, and the Woman Who Held Me On Her Lap.

She puts stuff in the Blue Car. She sits next to me. The Blue Car travels.

22. THE RANCH

Cedar Creek, Texas, ranch house

"Out." The Blue Car. I am in the grass. Short grass and tall grass. New smells. I smell mice. I smell bugs. I smell a scorpion.

I smell The Blue Car. The Blue Car is our home, The Woman Who Takes Me For Long Walks, The Man With Whom I Hunt, and me. I inspect a porch. I inspect a ranch house. The man and woman move stuff to a bedroom. My bed. I eat. I smell. I poop.

Another car. More people, The Man Who Tries Everything and the Woman With the Soft Touch. They eat. I eat. They sleep. I sleep. I sleep, a dog ball, in the bed with the Man with Whom I Hunt and The Woman Who Feeds Me.

The sun shines through the tall windows. I wake up, The Woman Who Feeds Me wake up. She feeds me. The Man With Whom I Hunt comes to the eating place and eats. The Man Who Tries Everything and the Woman With the Soft Touch greet me.

The Woman Takes Me For Long Walks puts on my harness and leash. I go through a big gate and down a street with grass, bushes, fences, and gates. Big Dogs come to see us. I greet the dogs. They escort us. I smell. I trot. I smell. I trot.

Lazy days at the ranch. I trot around the yard, I smell, I track interesting smells. I rest.

Sometimes I lie here. I remember The Man Who Trained Me, The Woman Who Fed Me, The Woman Who Held Me On Her Lap. I remember. Tears in my heart.

23. The Wedding

Lost Pines Resort and Spa, Cedar Creek, Texas
Mary goes away to fly home

We travel in the Blue Car. In a parking lot. I am on the leash. We walk by a river. I look over the river. I smell the river and hints of river creatures. I hunt in the long grass. I hunt in the bushes. 

I am in the Blue Car. "We'll be back." "We'll be back." The Woman Who Takes Me for Long Walks and The Man With Whom I Hunt disappear among the cars. I am alone. They will come back.

Night comes. I sleep. I wait. I look around. I bark. I wait.

The Man With Whom I Hunt is coming back to me. "Out." I jump. I Jump. I lick. "This way." In the grass. I smell. I hunt. This is who I am. This is who I am. This is who I am.

I am on a sidewalk. On the leash. We walk into a building. People here and there. A few greet me. I dog here and there. We look. I smell. We go into a small room. The doors shut. It goes up, rattle, rattle. I am used to the moving rooms. The doors open. We walk. A room. More people.

Back in the Blue Car. The Man With Whom I Hunt says, "I'll be back." I see him disappear among the cars. I wait. It gets dark. I wait. I wait. I wait too long. Will he come back? I wait. I wait. I wait. My heart beats fast.

The Man With Whom I Hunt appears out of the darkness. Oh joy. "Out." Oh Joy. I jump. I lick. I jump. I lick. He picks me up. I lick. My heart beats fast. He puts me down. "This way." I hunt. I hunt. I hunt. This is who I am. This is who I am. This is who I am.

I am on the leash. We walk in the night, on sidewalks, grass, through buildings. I smell traces of people and dogs.

We come to a building. Flashing lights shine through the glass. I hear loud music. People are wiggling. Lights are flashing. We go through glass doors. I walk through their moving feet. It is loud. We leave through the glass doors.

We walk in the dark, me and the Man With Whom I Hunt. I walk through parking lots. I walk through grass, the smell of people who were once here. The smell of dogs who were once here. I smell bugs. I smell worms in the soil.

I am in a parking lot. The Blue Car flashes lights. The Man With Whom I Hunt opens the door. "Up." I jump up. I am in the seat of The Woman Who Feeds Me. The Woman Who Feeds Me is not in her seat. Her scent lingers. This is her spot. I am in her seat. The Blue Car travels in the night.

24. A Blue Car Called Home

Cedar Creek, ranch

I am at the ranch house. The Woman Who Feeds Me is not here. The Woman Who Feeds Me is not here. The Man With Whom I Hunt sleeps. I sleep in a dog ball.

The sunlight shines through the window. I get up. People are up. I eat.

I am on the back porch. I look around me. I remember the night. Where is The Woman Who Feeds Me? Where is The Woman Who Takes Me for Long Walks?

I sprint. I gallop. I gallop to The Blue Car place. The Blue Car is here. Her smell is here. It is her home, The Woman Who Takes Me for Long Walks. It is her home that travels. It is my home. I smell. I know. I smell. She will come back to the Blue Car. I smell. I smell the lingering scent.

I hunt in the grass. I smell the scents of snakes who have been here. I do not wander far into the tall grass.

The Man With Whom I Hunt takes me for a trot. Big Dogs come to see us. They escort us through their neighborhood. I greet the dogs. There is grass and bushes by the road. I smell. I trot. I smell. I trot.

The people eat. I eat. I smell scorpions.

The sun has left the sky. I wait. I lie here. I wait. I remember The Man Who Trained Me, The Woman Who Fed Me, The Woman Who Held Me On Her Lap. I remember. Tears in my heart.

I remember The Woman Who Takes Me for Long Walks. Her smell is still here. She will not leave me forever.

The Man With Whom I Hunt sleeps. I sleep.

The sunlight shines through the window. I get up. People are up. I eat.

The Woman Who I Remember takes me for a trot. Big Dogs come to see us. They escort us through their neighborhood. I greet the dogs. I smell. I trot. I smell. I trot. They eat. I eat. I smell scorpions.

The sunlight shines through the window. I get up. People are up. I eat.

The Man With Whom I Hunt and The Woman Who I Remember put stuff in the Blue Car. The Woman Who I Remember sits in the seat that I sat in. I am in my go place. We travel.

22. LIZARDS AGAIN

Victoria, Texas, Tesla Charging Station

We stop. The Man With Whom I Hunt, The Woman Who I Remember in The Blue Car. "Out." I hunt. I smell. I smell a lizard. I stick my nose in the bushes. It moves, it scuttles. A lizard. I hunt. It scuttles. I hunt. This is who I am. This is who I am. This is who I am. Lizards, scuttle. I jump. Scuttle. I stick my nose in the bushes. Scuttle. Too fast for me — this time.

26. My Parking Lot

Port Aransas, Texas, Emilia's Landing Hotel

We stop. "Out." I get out. I am in a parking lot with rooms around it. I see a porch and more rooms on one side of the parking lot. I look around. I smell. This is a nice parking lot.

I smell, dogs, cats, mice, bugs, tobacco, people, I smell what was here. I smell every corner. I inspect. The people take stuff out of the Blue Car. We are staying here. This is my parking lot.

I trot around the parking lot. People standing on the porch greet me. I smell what was old cigarettes. I smell old oil drips. I smell where dogs and cats have been. I inspect.

The Man With Whom I Hunt leave the parking lot. "This way." I trot. On the sidewalks, across the street, in the grass and sand.

I am off the leash, in an alley. I smell the old scent of a skunk. I flip on my back and do the Back Dance, wiggle, wiggle, wiggle. I smell one with the skunk.

Port Aransas, Texas, Emilia's Landing Hotel, Flying Tigers Room. Shower stall.

The Man With Whom I Hunt pours water over me. He rubs soap and stuff in my fur. I get a shower. He rubs soap my fur. I get a shower. He rubs soap in my fur. I get a shower.

I smell like water and soap. I shake. He puts a towel over me and rubs my fur. I shake. Water flies off my fur. I shake.

I gallop out of the door. I inspect the parking lot. I smell. I smell. I smell. I greet people in the parking lot.

"Hazel." I trot to the Man Who Now Feeds Me.

We walk. I hunt. The salty breeze ruffles my fur. I smell what was here, dogs, cat, a mouse, bugs in the grass. This is who I am. This is who I am. This is who I am.

I eat. I drink.

The Man Who Now Feeds Me and The Woman Who I Remember sleep, one in each bed. I lie down.

I remember the old hunts. I remember The Man Who Trained Me, The Woman Who Fed Me, and the Woman Who Held Me On Her Lap. Tears in my heart.

27. BEACH DOG

Port Aransas, Texas, Sand Fest

I am on the leash. The Woman Who I Remember leads me. The Man With Whom I Hunt walks beside her. The wind is blowing, ruffling my fur. She leads me to a sand pile, a sculpted sand pile.

She leads me to another. Then another. The sculpted sand piles don't move. They smell like sand. I turn to look a the sand dunes. The sun is getting low in the sky. The sky is orange.

I see pelicans gliding above dunes. They are too far away to smell. I smell the salt. I smell the sand and the scent of seaweed coming from the waves.

"Up." We go back to my parking lot. I eat. We sleep.

Mustang Island, Texas

The Blue Car travels on the sand. We stop. "Out." The wind is blowing. The waves splash against the sand. I watch. I don't like the waves splashing on my paws.

The Man With Whom I Hunt runs. I gallop. I canter. I gallop. We run in a circle. The smell salt air, hints of sea creatures of all kinds fill my nose. The gentle roar of the waves, the sound of the wind fills my ears.

We circle. I jump. I bark. We run. Joy in the wind. I jump. I gallop. This is who I am. I smell the creatures of the sea and sand. This is who I am. This is who I am.

28. I WALK AROUND A PORT

Port Aransas, Texas

We wake up. I eat. The Man With Whom I Hunt takes me for a walk. I am on the leash. One the sidewalk I greet a dog. I smell the grass. I smell cooked food when we pass a building. We cross a parking lot. I smell old shrimp and potatoes. I see gulls and grackles eating.

We stop at land boats. They have plants and shells in them. We walk, I smell. We stop at land boats.

Port Aransas, Texas, Emilia's Landing Hotel

I eat. We sleep. I remember the wild beach. It is new to me. I am learning. I remember the learning to hunt in the mountains and forest in my puppy days. I sleep. I dream. I sleep.

The Man Who Now Feeds Me and The Woman Who I Remember put stuff in the Blue Car. We are going. I am not ready. I am not ready. I need to say goodbye. I inspect the parking lot. I smell. I inspect. I smell. People in the porch call to me. I look up. I smell. I inspect.

"Come." "Come." I trot to the Blue Car. "Up." "In your go place." The Blue Car travels.

I look out the window as the buildings go by.

29. A PLACE WHERE PEOPLE COME AND GO

Austin Airport

We are back at the busy street. Cars, people, stuff every-where. The Woman Who I Remember gets stuff out the Blue Car. She says goodbye to me. The Blue Car travels.

30. A GUEST IN ANOTHER DOG'S HOME

Round Rock, Texas

We stop. The Man With Whom I Hunt gets stuff out of the Blue Car. "Out." We go to the door. The Woman Who Has a Dog welcomes me in. I smell, I smell, I smell The Dog Who's Not Here. I smell The Dog Who's Not Here. I must be a guest of the The Dog Who's Not Here. I feel welcome here.

44

31. THE SQUIRREL EXCEPTION

I run to a door in the back. It has a window. I see grass. I see trees. I see squirrels! But, door is closed. I watch the squirrels. I cannot hunt the squirrels.

The Man With Whom I Hunt takes me for a walk, on the leash. We walk down sidewalks. I meet a dog. We walk across a bridge. There is a river, water, mud, bushes. I smell the creatures of the mud and bushes. We walk to a trail, grass, trees next to the river.

I am off the leash. "This way." We hunt. I hunt. I hunt. This is who I am. This is who I am. This is who I am. "Come." I gallop to The Man With Whom I Hunt.

"This way." We hunt. I hunt. I hunt. This is who I am. This is who I am. This is who I am. I smell. I see. A squirrel! I squirrel sprint.

"Come." "Come." I hear. I don't come. I must hunt the squirrel. The squirrel runs. I gallop. "Come." I must hunt the squirrel. The squirrel runs up a tree. I stop. I look up. I hope. I look up. I hope. The squirrel is on a branch. The squirrel is looking at me. I stare. The squirrel stares. The squirrel got away — this time.

"Come." "Come." I trot to The Man With Whom I Hunt.

We go back to the house of the Dog Who's Not Here. I sit on the couch. I lie on the couch.

32. A Snake in the Grass

I am in the backyard of The Other Dog's Home. I am on the leash. I smell. I hunt. I smell. Something in the bushes. I put my nose in the bush to smell better.

Danger. I slowly back up. Danger. A snake sticks his head up and watches me. I back up. I back up. I back up.

Lazy days. I wander through the house. The Woman Who Has a Dog, The Man Who Smells Like The Texas Hills welcome me. I sit on the couch when they sit on the couch. I look out the window. I eat.

The Man With Whom I Hunt takes me to the squirrel place. I trot. I stop and smell. I walk with my nose to the ground. I smell those the were once here, dogs, squirrels, cats, people, deer. I see no squirrels today.

The people eat. I eat. I sit on laps. I smell the Other Dog who is not here. I look through the glass in the back door. I see deer. I see ducks. I see squirrels.

We sleep. Sometimes I dream of the old hunts.

The Man With Whom I Hunt puts stuff in the Blue Car. I run out. Take me with you. "Up." "In your go place." I look out the window. The Woman Who Has a Dog, The Man Who Smells Like The Texas Hills wave at us.

The Blue Car travels.

33. A House

Oklahoma City

The Blue Car is next to a house. The Man Who Now Feeds Me moves stuff into the house. This must be our new home. I inspect. I smell the scent of critters have been in the yard.

The house welcomes me.

We go for a walk along the sidewalk. I smell the grass.

We walk back to the house. I run in the yard of the house next door. I smell a cat that was just here. "Hazel." I come back.

The Man With Whom I Hunt takes stuff from the car into the house. I am in the driveway. I sniff at the back door at the house next door. I smell a cat. The cat comes through a small door. I found the cat. The cat hisses and swipes at me with his paw. I back away. The Man With Whom I Hunt appears. "Hazel. Come." "Leave the cat alone."

We sleep. I eat.

34. My Fan Club

Oklahoma City, Oklahoma City Writer's Conference

We travel in the Blue Car to a big building. It has big sliding doors. I am on the leash. People everywhere. A woman pets me. "Cute." A man holds his hand to me. "Cute."

A woman pets me. "Cute." I sit. I lie on a couch. We walk. People say, "Cute." People stop and look at me. "Cute."

A room full of people in chairs. Feet, shoes, legs surround me. I sit on The Man With Whom I Hunt's lap. I look around. I wait. Shuffle, shuffle, shuffle, the people leave. I am on the leash. I trot out to the hallways. People look at me. "Cute." A man reached down to pet me. "Cute."

We go to our new home next to the Cat with Claws. We eat. We sleep. We wake up and go see my fan club.

People stop me and pet me. I get treats. They rub behind my ears. They say how cute I am.

35. DIGGING FOR GOPHERS

Wichita, Kansas

"Out." I am it the field with holes in it. I smell gophers under the ground. I stick my nose in the a hole. I stick my nose in another hole. I smell a gopher. I dig. I hunt. I dig. I hunt. I dig. I hunt. The smell of gopher fades into the tunnels under the ground. The gopher got away — this time.

36. FROM THE PLAINS TO THE SNOW

Hays, Kansas through Cheyenne, Wyoming

Stuff in the Blue Car. Are we leaving? Arc we leaving? "Up." "In your go place."

We travel in the Blue Car. We travel. We stop. I eat, I poop, I hunt. We stop. I eat, I poop, I hunt. I lie in a new bed.

The Blue Car rests. Around the White and Red Pillars I run. The Blue Car rattles and hums. I pace around White and Pillars. The Blue Car purrs. I circle around The Red and White Pillars. The Pillars hum. The Blue Car hums. I run around the car.

I am in the grass, in the bushes. The wind blasts through my fur. "This way." I smell, I hunt. I hunt. I hunt. This is who I am. This is who I am. This is who I am. My hunting heart is bright. This is who I am. This is who I am. This is who I am. I gallop in the wind. I gallop to The Man With Whom I Hunt.

Sometimes the Man leaves. I watch. I watch. When he comes back to the Blue Car, I jump for joy.

I wonder when I will see The Woman Who Takes Me For Long Walks. I wait.

We sleep. I dream of the hunts with The Man Who Trained Me, the kindness of the The Woman Who Fed Me, and the The Woman Who Held Me On Her Lap.

The sun shines through the window. I get out of bed. I eat. I poop. The Man Who Now Feeds me puts stuff in the Blue Car. "Up."

The Blue Car travels. The Blue Car rests. "Out." I see the tall grass. The wind is blowing fast through my fur. There are wave moving in the tall grass. I trot into the waves of tall grass. I canter. I canter. I canter. Joy in wind. Joy in the waves of grass. I canter. I gallop. I canter.

Billings, Montana

"Out." It is cold. It's snowing. I walk. I trot. It is too cold to smell. I shiver. "Come." I trot to The Man With Whom I Hunt, to the Blue Car. I stand. I look. I shake the snow off my fur.

"Up." "Get in your go place." The Blue Car travels. Snow falls on the windows. The Blue Car blows warm air on my fur. The Blue Car travels. We stop. We sleep.

I wake up. We go to the Blue Car. It's cold. It's windy. It's snowing. I shake the snow off my fur. I am cold. We travel.

37. My Favorite Door

Livingston, Montana

It is snowing. It is windy.

I have my paws on the glass. My favorite door. I look through. I like this window. I like this window in the door. The door opens, we go through. I am on the leash. I know where to go.

Another door, a metal door. A New Woman opens the metal door. The little room. The Man puts the stuff in the room. The Man motions. I go in the little room.

I stand looking up — The room goes up. Up, rattle, up. Up, rattle, up. The room moves. Rattle, stop. The door opens. "Out." We walk, the Man pulling stuff.

Another door. We are in a big room, with a bed, couch, furniture. I smell, I smell, I inspect. This is a temporary home. I jump on the couch, lie down. I watch. I wait. I wait. I wait. The next thing will come. I'm with him. I with the Blue Car. I lie here, peace in my heart.

38. The Blue Car Goes Home

Stuff in the Blue Car. "Up." "In your go place." I sit here. I lie here. We travel.

Hamilton, Montana

I know this street. I know this house. The Blue Car stops. The Blue Car has brought me to my Familiar Home. "Out."

There she is. There she is, The Woman Who Takes Me for Long Walks. There she is. I sprint to her. I jump. I jump.

The Man With Whom I Hunt and the Woman Who Takes Me For Long Walks pick me up. I am between them. They hug me. I lick. I wiggle. I lick.

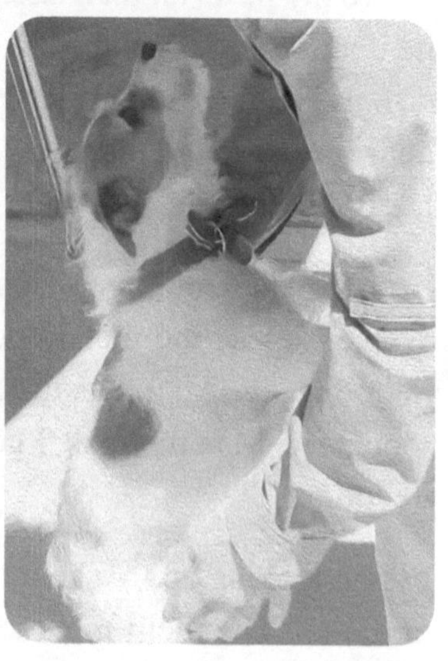

I am in my yard. I smell. I inspect. I am with them. I am with them, The Man With Whom I Hunt, The Woman Who Takes Me for Long Walks. I inspect the yard. I wander through the house. I am in my Familiar Home. I am with them. I gallop, joy in my heart.

Now, it is quiet in the night. I am with The Man With Whom I Hunt, The Woman Who Takes Me for Long Walks.

I lie here. I think of them who never came back, The Man Who Trained Me, The Woman Who Fed Me, The Woman Who Held Me On Her Lap. I remember.

I remember. I remember. Sweet tears in my heart.

Signed: **A Dog Called Hazel**

Translator's Epilogue

It was Saturday, a couple of days after Hazel and I returned home to Hamilton. As I often do, I rode my bike to downtown Hamilton to the Farmers Market. When I got back, Mary said Hazel had been run through with a pitchfork. They had gone to visit Ozzy and, as the dogs always do, had a rambunctious meeting for a couple of minutes. Hazel ran into an upturned pitchfork, two tines slicing through her flesh near each shoulder.

Mary said Hazel yelped and stumbled. Mary cleaned the wound and bandaged it. Hazel could walk, quietly bearing the first aid. But all the vets were closed in Hamilton. We traveled 45 miles to an emergency pet clinic in Missoula. Luckily, the tines didn't penetrate the chest cavity. The vets closed the wounds, stitching the wound in one shoulder.

They gave us antibiotics and a pain killer and told us to leave her kenneled for a week with five-minute leashed walk. After one round of pain killers, I watched her walk. She didn't seem to be in pain. We forewent the pain meds so Hazel could react to any pain and not hurt herself.

As to the kenneling, Hazel was having none of it. We just made sure she didn't run for a few days and took it easy.

When Mary took Hazel to her regular vet to get the stitches out, they were surprised. The stitches were gone. Hazel had taken them out with her teeth. To take a line from the movie *Wild At Heart,* Hazel is still dangerously cute, a tough dog with a kind heart, though when it comes to squirrels, lizards, or gophers it is she who is wild at heart.

The end

9 781734 233247